Minty and

Monty the sheepdog chased his brother Skip into the middle of the room. Just then, something caught his eye. Something white and woolly. It was huddled by the fire, as if it was about to pounce on him. He knew what it was—it was a lamb.

"Help!" Monty woofed.

Jenny Dale's Best Friends

Best ♥ Friends

Minty and Monty

by Jenny Dale
Illustrated by Susan Hellard

A Working Partners Book

Troll

Special thanks to Narinder Dhami

First U.S. edition published in 2003.

Text copyright © 2002 by Working Partners Limited.

Illustrations copyright © 2002 by Susan Hellard.

Best Friends is a trademark of Working Partners Limited.

Published by Troll Communications L.L.C.

Reprinted by arrangement with Macmillan Children's Books, London.

ISBN 0-8167-7513-3

Printed in Canada.

10 9 8 7 6 5 4 3 2 1

Chapter one

Whooooo-oooo!

"What's that noise, Mom?" whimpered Monty. The sheepdog puppy snuggled closer to his mother. They were lying in their warm basket in the farmhouse kitchen.

"It's just the wind," woofed his mom, Fern. She gently licked Monty's thick black-and-white fur. "It's nothing to be scared of."

The wind whistled down the chimney

again, making Monty shiver. He was glad he wasn't outside in the cold.

"Come and play, Monty," barked his brother, Skip. He was chasing a little rubber ball that Mrs. Johnson, the farmer's wife, had thrown for him.

"No, thanks," Monty woofed. He didn't much like playing with his brother. Skip was bigger and stronger than he was. His games were often too rough for Monty.

Suddenly the door crashed open. A gust of cold air blew into the kitchen, rattling the dishes on the plate rack. Mr. Johnson stood in the doorway, holding something wrapped in an old sack.

Monty whimpered in fear. He dived

behind his mom and hid his head under his paws.

The lamb in Mr. Johnson's arms pushed her head out of the sack and looked around. Minty could tell she wasn't out in the cold, windy fields anymore. Wherever she was, it was warm and sheltered. Not far away, she could see two of the farmer's sheepdogs, a big one and a little one. The little one was asleep. Minty's mom had told her all about sheepdogs. They sounded a bit scary.

"Maa-maa!" Minty felt very confused. She wanted her mom.

"One of the sheep is sick," Mr. Johnson explained to his wife. "This is her lamb. She's only two days old, so I think we'd better keep her indoors for a while. She can go back to the flock as soon as her mom is better." He handed Minty to Mrs. Johnson, and he went outside again.

Minty struggled to get out of the sack. She felt cold and sleepy, and the sack was itchy.

"Poor little thing," Mrs. Johnson said. "You need warming up." She wrapped the lamb in a cozy blanket so that only her fluffy white head was sticking out. Then she gently laid Minty on a big pillow beside the bright yellow fire.

"You'll need a friend if you're going to stay here for a while," said Mrs. Johnson.

"I wonder if you'd like Monty?" she asked, looking over at the puppy, who seemed to be hiding.

Minty was too tired to think about anything. She opened her mouth wide and yawned. Then she snuggled down in the blanket and fell asleep.

"Come on, Monty!" Skip nosed around behind his mom and nipped playfully at his brother's tail. "What are you hiding there for?"

"I'm *not* hiding," Monty yapped angrily. "I was just resting."

"You ran behind Mom when Mr. Johnson came in," Skip woofed. "You're scared of *everything*, Monty!"

"No, I'm not!" Monty yelped, trying to look brave. He jumped to his paws and marched out from behind his mom. "I'll show *you!*"

He chased Skip into the middle of the room. Just then, something caught his eye. Something white and woolly. And it was huddled beside the fire, as if it was about to pounce on him. . . .

"Help!" Monty woofed. He jumped backward and almost fell head over heels. "There's a strange animal in here!" He dashed over to his mom as fast as his paws could carry him.

Skip stared at his brother. "Don't be silly, Monty," he barked. "It's only a lamb! How are you ever going to be a good sheepdog if you're scared of a tiny lamb?"

"Skip's right, Monty." Fern nudged him with her black nose. "You know Mr. Johnson wants you both to learn how to herd the sheep."

"I've been out in the fields already," Skip boasted. "And I've watched Mom working with Mr. Johnson. It'll be *your* turn soon, Monty!"

Monty stared at the sleeping lamb. He wasn't looking forward to learning how to be a sheepdog. He hadn't started his training yet because he'd been sick when he was born. Monty was still getting well and strong. But maybe it wouldn't be so hard to be a sheepdog if he could start with just one lamb.

"Go and say hello to her, Monty," Skip barked. "I *dare* you!"

"Now, Skip," woofed Fern. "Don't tease your brother."

Skip ran off to find his ball. Meanwhile, Monty sat and stared at the lamb. He was longing to get a closer look. Maybe he could, if he crept across the kitchen really quietly. . . .

He sneaked over to the kitchen table and hid behind one of the chairs. He peered out. The lamb was still asleep. Monty crept slowly across the floor and crouched behind Mrs. Johnson's knitting basket. He was getting closer!

And the lamb was *still* asleep.

Hardly daring to breathe, Monty went

right up to the pillow. The lamb didn't look scary at all now. Her eyes were tightly shut, and Monty could hear her breathing softly as she slept. Monty thought she must have been cold outside. Feeling very brave, he leaned over and gave the lamb a gentle lick on the nose.

Suddenly Minty opened her eyes.

"Ma-a-a!" she bleated loudly, and she sat up.

"Oh!" Monty was taken by surprise. He dashed away and hid behind Mrs. Johnson's rocking chair. After a moment, he peeped around the side of it.

The lamb and the puppy stared at each other.

"Who are you?" Minty bleated. She was feeling wide awake after her nap. She looked at the little sheepdog. He had thick black fur and a white patch on his nose. He was much too small to be scary.

Monty didn't say anything for a moment. He looked at the lamb's soft woolly coat, her long thin legs, and her small black nose. "I'm Monty," he woofed at last.

"My name's Minty, I think," replied the lamb. She looked around. "Where am I?"

"You're in the farmhouse," Monty explained. He felt quite safe in his place behind the rocking chair.

"I want to look around!" Minty bleated. She wriggled her way out of the blanket and hopped off the pillow. Her legs felt a bit wobbly at first, and it took her a moment to get her balance. Then she trotted off to explore.

Monty watched the lamb as she poked her nose into Mrs. Johnson's knitting basket and sniffed the dogs' water bowl. She didn't seem scared of *anything*, he thought.

Minty decided that she liked being in the farmhouse. It was cozy and warm. It would be a good home until she could go back to her mom and the rest of the flock. Her mother had told her that sheepdogs were supposed to tell sheep what to do. This puppy looked as if he was scared of his own shadow! But it would be fun to have someone to play with.

"I'm going to be living here for a while," Minty bleated. "Will you be my friend?"

Monty wasn't sure. He backed away from her, his ears flat against his head.

"Oh, come on!" Minty bounded over to him playfully. "It'll be fun."

Suddenly Monty realized the lamb was

much taller than he was. She might want to play rough games the way Skip did. Feeling very worried, Monty wriggled out from under the chair and darted across the kitchen.

"Good idea! Let's play tag!" Minty rushed after him, her shiny black hooves tapping on the kitchen floor. "I'll bet I can catch you!"

Monty didn't turn around. He jumped into the dog basket and buried his head behind his mom's warm body.

Skip stopped chewing his ball and watched in amazement. "A *lamb* chasing a *sheepdog!*" he woofed. "I don't believe it."

Chapter Two

It was the following morning. Minty jumped off her pillow and stretched. "I'm hungry!" she bleated. She pattered across the slippery kitchen floor and butted her head against Mrs. Johnson's legs. "Hurry up with my milk!"

The farmer's wife was pouring warm milk into a bottle. She fixed on a rubber nipple and sat down in the rocking chair, lifting Minty onto her lap.

Monty opened one eye. He had been

warm and cozy next to his mom during the night. Now Fern and Skip had gone out into the fields. Monty decided to stay in the basket for a few more minutes. He was hungry, but he didn't want the lamb to chase him again.

"Mmm!" Minty bleated happily as she

began to drink the warm milk. Her tail wagged quickly back and forth.

Monty poked his head over the side of the basket. He loved milk. Maybe there would be a few drops left over for him.

"Hello there!" Minty bleated, catching sight of Monty's soft black nose. "Would you like to share my milk?"

Monty's empty tummy rumbled at the thought. He began to wag his tail. "Yes, please!" he woofed. He jumped out of the basket and ran over to the rocking chair.

Mrs. Johnson patted Monty and lifted him onto her lap. It was a little crowded, but the lamb's soft fleece felt nice and warm against Monty's fur.

Monty waited patiently until Minty had finished sucking at the bottle. Then he stretched over and grabbed the rubber nipple with his teeth. Mrs. Johnson laughed and poured the rest of the milk into a saucer on the floor for him.

When he had finished, Mrs. Johnson put the lamb down next to him. Minty looked around the kitchen. Mr. Johnson had gone out to feed the chickens, leaving the door open.

"Let's go out into the farmyard," Minty suggested.

"Okay!" Monty woofed. He really liked Minty now that she had shared her milk with him. He followed her out into the sunshine. The ducks on the pond cackled loudly at them. "Watch out for those ducks!" yapped Monty. "They can be fierce!"

"Don't worry about those silly old things," Minty bleated. "Look, the barn door is open. Let's go inside!"

"Do you think we should?" Monty yelped. He'd never been in the barn before. Mr. Johnson usually kept the big doors shut.

"Don't worry." Minty ran across the yard, her fuzzy tail wagging. She loved exploring. "I'll take care of you!" She poked her head into the barn and looked around. Mr. Johnson's tools and machinery were stacked on both sides, and there was a big heap of straw in the middle.

"Is it scary?" Monty yapped from out in the yard.

"No, not at all!" Minty bleated. "Come on." She trotted into the barn and dived into the pile of straw. Then she rolled onto her back with her legs in the air. The straw felt warm, and it made a nice crunchy sound.

Monty thought that Minty looked as if she was having fun. He took a deep breath and scampered into the barn. With a loud woof, he leaped onto the heap of straw.

"Oink! Oink! Oink!"

The pile of straw moved underneath him. Monty howled with fright. A pair of pink ears popped up beside him, followed by two small eyes and a long, fat snout.

"If you don't mind!" the pig grunted angrily. "Some of us are trying to sleep!"

Minty jumped up and faced the pig. "Sorry," she bleated. "We didn't see you."

Monty could feel his heart pounding. "Let's go," he whined in Minty's ear.

"Why?" Minty bleated. "Let's make friends!"

"Oink! No, thanks. I'd rather get some sleep!" the pig grunted. He shook himself and settled down under the straw again.

Minty tossed her head and trotted out of the barn.

Monty hurried after his friend and gave her a quick lick. He couldn't believe how brave she was. She hadn't even been scared of that grumpy old pig!

They stopped at the edge of the farmyard. Monty could see Skip herding some sheep into the paddock as Mr. Johnson and Fern watched him. Skip darted from side to side behind the sheep and didn't let any of them get away. The farmer looked very pleased with him.

Monty stared miserably at the sheep. They frightened him. They were a lot bigger than Minty, with huge, woolly coats that wobbled and shook when they ran. And there were so *many* of them. He would never be able to tell them what to do! "I wish I wasn't a sheepdog at all!" Monty woofed gloomily.

In the paddock, Skip barked sharply as one of the sheep started to wander off. The sheep bleated loudly and ran back to the flock.

Monty looked at the lamb beside him, feeling puzzled. "Don't the sheep get frightened when the sheepdog chases them?" he asked.

"No, of course not," Minty replied. "My mom says that the sheepdog is there to help us."

Suddenly, two of the sheep broke away and galloped across the paddock toward them. Monty howled in fright. The sheep looked very fierce! He was about to turn and run when Minty stopped him.

"It's all right, Monty," she bleated quickly. "They're my aunts!"

"Baa! Hello there!" bleated the biggest sheep. She pushed her head through the paddock fence. "We wanted to let you know that your mom is feeling better today."

"Yes, you should be back in the field with us very soon," the other one added.

"Oh, great!" Minty answered happily. She stretched up and touched noses with the sheep.

But Monty kept well back from the fence. Even though these two sheep sounded friendly, they were still *big*. They had long noses and big yellow eyes. . . .

"Come on now, ladies," Skip barked, bounding up to them. "Time to go!"

"We're coming," bleated the first sheep. "I don't know," she continued, turning to her sister, "why these young pups are so impatient!"

"I'm just trying to do my job properly!" Skip barked. As the sheep trotted off, he turned to his brother. "Oh, by the way, Monty, Mr. Johnson says you'll be starting your training really soon. Isn't that great?" And he ran after the sheep.

Monty was so shocked he couldn't say anything.

Minty looked at him anxiously. "It won't be that bad, Monty," she bleated. She couldn't understand why Monty was so scared. After all, he *was* a sheepdog. "You'll be fine."

Monty didn't answer. He didn't want to go out onto the windy hillside and learn how to herd the big, scary sheep. He wanted to stay safe in the farmyard with Minty forever.

Chapter Three

"Monty! *Monty!*" Minty raced around the kitchen looking for her friend. "Where *are* you?"

"Under here." Monty crept out from beneath the china cabinet. There were cobwebs all over his black fur.

"Oh, *Monty!*" the little lamb bleated. "You can't hide. Mr. Johnson will come looking for you soon."

"I know," Monty whimpered, his ears drooping. Today was the day he was going to start his training.

"I'll be going back to my flock today, now that my mom's feeling better," Minty bleated.

Monty's ears drooped even more. "I'll miss you," he snuffled sadly.

"I know." Minty looked sad, too. "I really want to see my mom and all my friends again, but I don't want to leave *you*."

"Maybe we can still play together sometimes," Monty woofed hopefully.

"Of course we can," Minty agreed, pressing her woolly body close to him. "I'll see you when you're herding the sheep, won't I?"

Monty didn't want to think about that.

Suddenly the kitchen door opened. Mr. Johnson stood there with Skip at his heels.

"Come on, Monty," Skip woofed. "It's your first day of training!" He walked bossily over to Minty. "And you've got to come along, too," he added. "You're going back to your flock today."

"You don't have to herd me," Minty replied boldly. "I know the way!" And she bounded over to the door.

Mr. Johnson whistled, and Monty trotted over to him. He felt like running off and hiding, but he knew he had to do what the farmer wanted. He trailed miserably behind his brother as they went outside.

Even though Minty was excited about

seeing her mom again, she couldn't help thinking about Monty. She paused when she got to the paddock and waited for her friend to catch up. "Don't worry, Monty," she said, licking his ear. "It's not that bad!"

There was a sound of bleating in the distance, and Minty turned her head eagerly. She could see Fern herding the sheep down the hillside. Minty caught sight of a familiar woolly face. "There's my mom!" she bleated in delight. Her tail wagged so fast it was just a blur. But before she ran into the paddock, she whispered in Monty's ear. "You can do it, Monty. I know you can!"

Monty watched as the lamb wriggled under the fence and skipped across the paddock. He knew Minty was just being kind. There was no way he could be a sheepdog. He watched in alarm as the sheep got closer and closer. Their hooves sounded like thunder. It felt as if a hundred yellow eyes were glaring at him. Shaking with fear, Monty crept toward Skip.

"Maa-maa!" Minty spotted her mother on the edge of the flock. She dashed over to her and rubbed her head against her warm, woolly side.

"I'm so glad you're back," her mom bleated. "I've missed you very much."

"And I'm glad you're better," Minty replied. "I met a really nice sheepdog when I was living in the farmhouse. His name's Monty. He's standing there by the fence."

Minty's mother looked around the paddock as Fern herded them through the gate. "I can't see him," she said.

"I think he's hiding," Minty explained. "He's afraid of the big sheep."

"Oh dear," Minty's mom bleated. "I

hope he's going to be all right. There are some very grumpy sheep in this flock— like old Dolly over there."

Dolly was walking at the back of the flock with her gang of friends. They kept trying to drop back, but as soon as they slowed down, Fern rounded them up and sent them forward again.

Minty and her mom trotted into the paddock. When most of the sheep had gone through the gate, Mr. Johnson whistled loudly.

"Go on, Monty," Skip barked. "That means you!"

"You can do it, if you like," Monty offered from his hiding place behind Skip. "I don't mind!"

"Monty!" Fern barked sternly at him. "Come here. You've got to herd the last group of sheep into the paddock!"

"Really?" Monty whimpered. Very slowly, with his head down and his ears flat, he trotted toward the last few sheep.

"Go on, Monty," Skip woofed. "Just show them who's boss!"

Well, it's not me! Monty thought. He felt so small next to those huge sheep.

A bony old ewe with mean eyes stared at him. "Look at this, girls!" she bleated scornfully. "Is this a real sheepdog, or is it a mouse?"

"Oooh, I think it's a mouse!" one of the other sheep answered rudely.

Minty watched them from the paddock.

"Stop that, Dolly!" she bleated angrily. "Leave him alone!" But none of the sheep were listening to her.

Monty was trembling so much he could hardly move. "Would you all go into the paddock, please?" he yapped, trying not to sound scared stiff.

The old ewe stared at him with her big yellow eyes. "And why should we?" she demanded. She stamped her foot, and the group of sheep scattered across the field.

Monty didn't know *what* to do. He stood there helplessly, watching them run all over the place.

Suddenly Mr. Johnson gave a loud whistle. Skip raced forward and rounded up the naughty sheep. They grumbled

noisily as he herded them into the paddock.

Monty hung his head in shame. Mr. Johnson looked angry. Even worse, Monty's mom looked disappointed.

"It's hopeless," Monty woofed sadly to himself. "I'm *never* going to be a real sheepdog!"

Chapter Four

"I'm sorry, Mom," Monty whimpered sadly. He pressed himself against his mother's warm furry body.

"Shh. Don't worry." Fern licked his drooping ears. "You'll get another chance tomorrow."

"But I don't *want* another chance!" Monty howled. "I'm never going to be a good sheepdog. Never!" He glanced over at his brother, who was standing beside Mr. Johnson, wagging his tail. *Why can't*

I be more like Skip? thought Monty.

Over in the paddock, Minty wriggled between the other sheep until she was at the edge of the flock. She could see that Monty was upset. She wanted to go and comfort him, but she knew that she had to stay in the paddock for now. "Poor

Monty," she bleated to her mom. "I wish I could help him."

Just then, Mr. Johnson whistled to Skip. It was time for the sheep to go back up the hillside. Minty saw her chance. As the sheep began to stream through the gate, she slipped away from the others. Monty didn't notice her as she ran across the field, but Minty could hear everything Fern was saying.

"Now, Monty, listen to me," barked his mom. "You have to learn how to herd the flock, or you won't be able to live here anymore."

Monty jumped in alarm. "Not live here anymore!" he yelped. "Why not?"

His mom nuzzled him gently with her

nose. "Well, Mr. Johnson has plans for you pups," she explained. "Skip is going to live with Mr. Brown, whose farm is on the other side of the hill."

"What about me?" Monty woofed in a small voice.

"Mr. Johnson wants to keep you for himself," his mother replied. "But you won't be much use to him if you can't herd the sheep."

"So what will happen to me, then?" Monty whimpered.

"I'm sure you'll go to a good home," his mom told him. "But you won't be a farm dog anymore."

Monty's tail drooped. He didn't want to leave the farm. It was his home. He didn't want to leave his mom either. And what about Minty, his best friend? He'd never see her again. . . .

"Oh no!" Minty bleated in alarm. She would really miss Monty if he was sent away. And she knew that Monty would miss her, too. *Maybe I can help him,* she thought, feeling very determined. She was just about to dash over to Monty when Skip appeared.

"Hurry up, Minty," he woofed. This was the first time Skip had been in charge of the whole flock. He was being even more bossy than usual. "You'll be left behind."

"But—" Minty protested.

"Come along, please." Skip nudged her

toward the other sheep. "You're holding everyone up."

Minty had no choice. She trotted over to join the rest of the flock, which was making its way up the hillside. "Don't worry, Monty," she bleated, looking back over her shoulder. "I haven't given up. I'm going to help you—somehow!"

Chapter Five

After the warm and cozy farmhouse, the hillside felt very cold. Minty spent the night cuddled against her mom's big woolly body. As soon as she woke up, she tried to think of a way to help Monty. At last she had an idea.

Minty knew that the sheep would be rounded up again this morning and taken down to the paddock for Monty's training. She bounded into the middle of the flock and looked around. "Listen to me!" she bleated as loudly as she could. "Listen to me, *everyone!*"

Most of the sheep turned around and stared at Minty. Only Dolly and her friends continued chatting away with each other.

"Be quiet!" Minty dashed over to the

little group and bravely pushed her way into the middle of them. "I want to talk to the whole flock!"

"What?" Dolly glared at the little lamb. "Why should we want to listen to *you?*"

"It's about my friend, Monty." Minty wasn't going to let Dolly stop her, now that the entire flock was listening. "You know, the sheepdog."

"Oh, yes, we know him!" Dolly bleated rudely. "He's the worst sheepdog we've ever seen!"

There were murmurs of agreement from some of the other sheep.

"He isn't!" Minty insisted. "I know he can be a good sheepdog. He just needs more practice."

"Why are *you* standing up for him?" asked one of the other sheep.

"Because he's my friend!" Minty replied. "He played with me when I was living in the farmhouse. None of the other dogs wanted to be my friend. Monty is special."

The sheep started muttering among themselves.

"All I want is for you to give him a chance," Minty bleated, looking around at them. "Just do what he wants."

Minty's mom joined in. "Isn't it better to have a kind, gentle sheepdog like Monty, rather than a grumpy, snappy one?"

A few of the sheep nodded as if they agreed. But Dolly and her friends still looked scornful. "If this pup can't be a good sheepdog on his own, he shouldn't be one at all!" Dolly said grumpily. And most of the flock bleated in agreement.

Minty didn't say any more. She'd done her best to make things easier for Monty. But it looked as though some of the sheep didn't want to help. . . .

Monty stood in the field, shaking. This was his last chance. He'd heard the farmer say so to Mrs. Johnson. If Monty didn't do any better today, he would be leaving the farm for good.

Fern and Mr. Johnson had gone up the hill to fetch the sheep. Skip was waiting in the paddock, and even Mrs. Johnson had come out of the farmhouse to watch.

Monty knew he was going to make a mess of herding the sheep again. His ears drooped as he saw the herd come streaming down the hillside. He looked at Mr. Johnson, waiting for the signal to start.

Fern brought the sheep into the field. Mr. Johnson gave a short whistle. Fern dropped to the ground and lay still.

Monty knew it was his job to herd the sheep through the gate and into the paddock. He started forward, his heart pounding. What was he supposed to do first? His ears drooped even more. He just didn't have a clue.

As soon as she saw Monty trotting gloomily across the field, Minty pushed her way out of the flock. She had come up with

one last idea to help her friend. "Monty!" she bleated at the top of her voice. "Run around to the side of the flock. Look for any sheep that are wandering off!"

Monty jumped when he heard the familiar bleat. It was Minty! He was very relieved to see his friend. He did exactly what she said. He scampered around behind the flock, keeping close to the ground the way his mom did. At once the straying sheep stopped going in a different direction and pressed themselves neatly back into the flock.

Monty stopped in surprise. He hadn't realized that if he ran toward the sheep they would go in the direction he wanted.

"Don't stop, Monty!" Minty bleated

urgently as the sheep began to head for the gate to the paddock. "You need to make sure no one gets left behind!"

Monty dashed back around the flock. He spotted a stray lamb wandering off. He ran toward it. "Come on, move along, please!" he barked.

The lamb bleated and trotted back to its mother. Monty ran toward the sheep again, and they walked right through the gate into the paddock. Suddenly Monty realized that this was what the sheep *expected* him to do. For the first time ever, Monty felt like a real sheepdog!

"How am I doing, Minty?" he woofed.

"Just great!" Minty bleated. She was already in the paddock with most of the other sheep. "Don't let the ones at the back get away. Keep an eye on them—especially that mean old Dolly!"

Feeling much happier, Monty raced off to round up the rest of the flock. Then his heart sank. Dolly and her friends were standing quite still in the middle of the field. And they were staring at him stubbornly with their fierce yellow eyes.

Chapter Six

Monty was worried. Quickly he glanced over at Minty for help.

"Don't be scared," she bleated. "Look, most of the sheep are in already! You can do it!"

Monty looked around. Minty was right. He'd herded nearly the whole flock into the paddock. Was he going to let Dolly and her gang stop him now? No, he wasn't! "Get into the paddock, please, ladies!" he barked.

"Aren't you going to ask us nicely?" Dolly answered rudely.

"I'm not asking you," Monty woofed. "I'm *telling* you!" And he ran toward the group of sheep without another thought.

Dolly and her friends were taken by surprise. Bleating and grumbling, they rushed forward, out of Monty's way and into the paddock.

Monty nosed the gate shut and then stood there, trembling all over. He'd done it!

"Great job, Monty!" His mom and Skip rushed over to cover him with licks. Mrs. Johnson started clapping, and even Mr. Johnson looked pleased.

"You need a lot more training, Monty," he said with a smile. "But I think one day

you'll be as good as your mom!" And he
patted Monty on his head.

Monty felt so proud he thought he
would burst. The farmer signaled to him
to herd all the sheep back out of the
paddock. This time Monty fearlessly
trotted over to the flock.

The sheep began to file out of the paddock without complaining. Monty hung back, looking for a familiar face. As soon as he spotted it, he bounded over. "Minty! Thanks for helping me herd the sheep. I couldn't have done it without you!"

"You did a great job!" Minty bleated happily, rubbing her head against her friend. "And now that you're a real sheepdog, we'll be able to see each other every day!"

"We'll still be best friends, won't we?" Monty woofed.

"Always," Minty replied.

"But you'll have to do what I say!" Monty reminded her.

"Will I?" Minty bleated. She jumped playfully around him and then skipped away across the field. "You'll have to catch me first!"

Snowflake and Sparkle

Snowflake is a puppy with big paws and soft, golden fur. His best friend is Sparkle—a very unusual kitten. She chases balls, scares the mailman, and begs for treats—just like a dog!

Snowflake longs to be more like Sparkle—but one day, the tiny kitten gets into BIG trouble. Can Snowflake come to the rescue?

ISBN 0-8167-7511-7

Available wherever you buy books.

Pogo and Pip

Pip the hamster loves his cozy little home. But when his cage door is left open, Pip sees the lovely green garden outside and decides to explore.

The big, wide world is full of danger for a tiny hamster. Soon Pip is running for his life! But a friendly guinea pig called Pogo is watching—will he be able to help?

ISBN 0-8167-7512-5

Available wherever you buy books.